THE LOST BALLOON

written by
KANA RILEY

illustrated by
RALPH YZNAGA

 **Macmillan McGraw-Hill**

New York   Farmington

2

Up goes the white balloon . . .

over the yellow cab . . .

over the red truck

and the black ladder . . .

under the
green bridge . . .

over the brown building . . .

into the big blue balloon.

Hooray!